Pogo and P̶i̶p̶

Pip squeaked with sur̶p̶r̶i̶s̶e̶ ̶̶̶ ̶̶̶d̶o̶or of his cage was open. He co̶u̶l̶d̶n̶'̶t̶ believe his eyes. How could that have happened?

He ran over to the cage door and peered around the kitchen. Pip could see the garden through the open back door. The sun was shining and the green grass looked juicy and tempting . . .

Jenny Dale's Best Friends

More Best Friends follow soon!

Best ♥ Friends

Pogo and Pip

by Jenny Dale
Illustrated by Susan Hellard

A Working Partners Book

MACMILLAN CHILDREN'S BOOKS

To Amanda and Jaclyn Wyzinski, with love

Special thanks to Narinder Dhami

First published 2002 by Macmillan Children's Books
a division of Pan Macmillan Limited
20 New Wharf Road, London N1 9RR
Basingstoke and Oxford
www.panmacmillan.com

Associated companies throughout the world

Created by Working Partners Limited
London W6 0QT

ISBN 0 330 39854 7

3 5 7 9 8 6 4 2

A CIP catalogue record for this book is available from
the British Library.

Typeset by SX Composing DTP, Rayleigh, Essex
Printed and bound in Great Britain by Mackays of Chatham plc, Kent

Chapter One

"Are we there yet, Rashid?" Pip the hamster squeaked loudly to his owner. Pip was so excited, he just couldn't stay still. He jumped on to his wheel and began to run round as fast as he could.

"Look, Pip." Rashid held up the cage so that the hamster could see out of the car window. "We're here! This is our new house."

Pip jumped eagerly off his wheel and ran to the side of the cage. He stood up on his back legs, his whiskers twitching, and peered through the window. Rashid had told him lots of times that they were leaving their old house and moving to a new one. Pip had been a bit nervous at first. He thought he might have to leave his cage behind as well!

Pip thought the new house looked very nice. It was much bigger than the old one, and it had a large garden all round it with lots of trees. The front door was open and removal men were carrying furniture and boxes inside.

"Don't leave me behind!" Pip squeaked anxiously, as Rashid and his family climbed out of the car. He couldn't *wait* to see inside the new house.

"Come on, Pip," said Rashid. "Let's go and explore." He picked up Pip's

cage from the back seat and tucked it
under his arm. He was already carrying
two bags filled with toys and his hands
were full. The cage lurched and Pip slid
across the floor.

"Here, let me give you a hand," said
one of the removal men.

Gratefully, Rashid handed Pip's cage
to the man.

"Hello, little hamster," the removal man said to Pip as he carried the cage up the garden path.

Pip sniffed curiously as they went inside. The new house smelt very different from the old one. He hoped that Rashid would let him out of his cage very soon, so that he could look around.

As soon as they were in the house, Rashid dashed upstairs. He must have gone to look at his new bedroom, Pip thought. In the old house, Rashid and Pip had shared a bedroom with Rashid's little brother, Hasim. Rashid had told Pip that they were going to have their very own bedroom now.

Pip was very pleased! Hasim didn't

understand that hamsters liked to snooze during the day and he was always noisy.

The removal man looked round the hall for somewhere to put Pip's cage.

"I want to go upstairs with Rashid!" Pip squeaked. But the man took no notice. He carried Pip's cage into the kitchen and put it down on the table with a thump.

"Careful!" Pip squealed in alarm.

The man hurried out of the back door into the garden. Pip couldn't help feeling a bit cross. He didn't want to be stuck in the kitchen on his own. Where was Rashid? Pip wished his owner would come and take him upstairs to see their new bedroom . . .

Suddenly Pip squeaked with surprise.

The door of his cage was open. He couldn't believe his eyes. How could that have happened? The latch must have come undone when the removal man put the cage down with a bump. Pip had never been out of his cage before without Rashid there to look after him.

He ran over to the cage door and peered around the kitchen. He could jump out and run upstairs to find Rashid. Or he could go and explore outside. Pip could see the garden through the open back door. The sun was shining and the green grass looked juicy and tempting. Rashid had taken Pip out into the garden several times at their old house. But was Pip brave enough to go outside on his own?

He stretched his nose upwards and sniffed the air. He could smell the fresh grass and sweet flowers on the breeze. "I'll do it!" he said to himself.

With his heart thumping, Pip hopped out of the cage. The table felt cold and smooth under his paws. He jumped carefully down on to the seat of a chair, and then on to the floor.

He paused for a moment, listening. He could hear voices in the hallway and people moving around upstairs. But no one came into the kitchen.

Pip scurried over to the back door and looked out. He could see birds sitting in the trees and butterflies fluttering around in the sunshine. He waited on the doorstep for a moment, wondering what to do. He was beginning to feel a bit scared. The garden was so big . . .

Suddenly there was the sound of heavy footsteps. With a startled squeak, Pip scrambled out of the back door, down the steps, and darted behind a big clump of yellow flowers. A moment later, two of the removal men came through the side gate carrying a big box.

Pip hoped the removal men wouldn't notice that his cage was empty. He knew Rashid would be worried if he thought that Pip was missing. "I'll be back before anyone notices I've gone," Pip promised himself. "I only want to have a little look around."

He scampered out from behind the flowers and ran into the middle of the lawn. The sun felt warm on his golden fur. "Come and play!" he squeaked to the birds who were sitting high up in the trees. But the birds took no notice of him.

Suddenly, a butterfly danced past Pip's nose, making him jump. "Hello," he squeaked, stretching up on his back paws. "Come and play."

The butterfly flapped its big soft wings, tickling Pip's nose. Then it flew across the garden and landed on a bright red flower at the edge of the lawn. Pip followed it. He spotted some seeds lying underneath the flower. He held one in this front paws and nibbled it.

"This is very tasty!" Pip squeaked happily. He had plenty of food in the

bowl in his cage, but these seeds were too good to resist. He began to nibble on another seed.

Suddenly, Pip stopped nibbling. He turned his head one way. Then he turned his head the other way. His whiskers twitched. Something felt very odd. He had the strangest feeling that he was being *watched* . . .

chapter Two

Pogo the guinea-pig had run out of things to do. He'd eaten some food and he'd drunk some water. He had been out in his run twice and he'd sat in the sunshine for a while. He'd just woken up from a lovely, long nap in his bed of hay, and now he felt a bit lonely. He couldn't wait for his owner, Chloe, to come back from school. Then she would play with him, like they did every day.

Bang! Crash!

Pogo lifted his smooth black head and

listened hard. He could hear strange
noises in next door's garden. Voices too.

"I wonder what's going on?" he
squeaked. He knew that the house next
door had been empty for a while. The
children who used to live there had been
Chloe's friends and they had often come
round to play with Pogo. But they had
moved away. So who was making all that
noise?

Pogo trotted out of his wooden hutch
into his run. The fence between the two
houses was made of wire mesh like his
run, so he could see right into the
garden next door.

He saw a man carrying boxes into the
kitchen. New people must be moving in,
thought Pogo. Two more men appeared

round the corner. One of them dropped the box he was carrying, and it landed on the other man's toe. The man yelled loudly, and dropped the box that *he* was carrying. Pogo thought it was all very funny.

But then he noticed something else. He blinked. What was that? Was he seeing things?

For a moment, Pogo thought he had seen a little golden hamster running across the lawn next door. He knew just what hamsters looked like. There had been lots in the pet shop where Pogo had lived before. But he also knew that hamsters lived in cages indoors. So there shouldn't be one in the garden.

"I must be dreaming," he squeaked.

But no! There it was again! Pogo's eyes
almost popped out of his head. There
was a hamster running around next-
door's garden.

Pogo watched the hamster snuffling
about in the grass and squeaking at the
birds. Then it chased a butterfly over to
the flowerbeds. It picked up some seeds
and began to nibble them. It didn't seem

a bit scared, Pogo thought. In fact, the hamster seemed very happy to be outside.

But suddenly Pogo spotted something else in the garden. Two big, green eyes were peering out from underneath a leafy bush. The eyes were fixed firmly on the little hamster.

"Oh no!" Pogo squeaked. He knew who it was. It was Doris, the big tabby cat who lived in the house at the bottom of his garden. The little hamster was in danger!

Chapter Three

Pogo didn't know what to do. The hamster hadn't noticed Doris at all. It was too busy munching the seeds. And any minute now, the cat would pounce . . .

"Hey, you!" Pogo put his paws up against the wire and squeaked as loudly as he could. "Look out!"

Pip was still tucking into his feast of seeds. Soon his tummy began to feel very full. He decided to fill his cheek pouches with some seeds to eat later.

"What's that noise?" he wondered, as he picked up another seed. He could hear a faint squeaking sound. He looked around and spotted a black and brown guinea-pig in the garden next door. The guinea-pig was running up and down his run, squeaking at the top of his voice. He seemed very worried about something.

"What *is* he doing?" Pip listened hard, still holding the seed.

Just then a shadow fell across him. Pip looked up and nearly jumped out of his skin. A huge tabby cat loomed over him, ready to scoop him up with one giant paw.

"Help!" Pip squeaked. He dropped the seed and tore across the grass towards the house.

The cat bounded after him. Pip dived behind a flowerpot at the edge of the lawn. But the cat stopped running too, and stared at Pip's hiding place with its fierce green eyes.

Safe in his run, Pogo watched in horror as the hamster dashed across the grass. He didn't know what he could do to help. Would the hamster get away from Doris?

Pip was very frightened. He couldn't get back into the kitchen because the cat was between the flowerpot and the back door. He looked behind him and saw the wire fence. He was just small enough to squeeze through, but the cat would be much too big. He took a deep breath and ran as fast as he could to the fence.

He wriggled through the mesh into the guinea-pig's garden.

But the cat ran straight after him. She leaped lightly up on to the fencepost and balanced there for a moment. She looked down at Pip, ready to jump down and grab him.

"You're not safe yet!" Pogo squeaked. "Quick, over here!" He had just

remembered something. There was a small hole in the wire in one corner of his run. It wasn't big enough for Pogo to squeeze through. But it was just big enough for a hamster.

"Over here!" Pogo squeaked again. He stood right by the hole and pushed it with his paw to make it as big as he could.

Pip realised what the guinea-pig was telling him. He dashed over to the run, just as the cat jumped down from the fence. He dived for the hole and pushed his way through. He was just in time.

A second later, the cat pounced, but her paws closed on thin air. "Miaow!" she hissed crossly.

Pogo looked down at the hamster. He

was lying on the grass, his sides heaving and his whiskers twitching like mad. Meanwhile, Doris was standing outside the run, glaring in at them.

"Are you all right?" Pogo asked the hamster, feeling very worried.

"Yes, I think so," Pip panted. He squeaked with fear and hid his head under his paws as the cat pushed her big face right up against the wire mesh. She looked very angry indeed.

"Come into my hutch," Pogo offered kindly. "Doris can't see us in there."

"Thank you," Pip squeaked, as he followed the guinea-pig inside. His legs were trembling so much he could hardly walk. "If it wasn't for you, I don't know *how* I would have got away."

"That's OK," Pogo squeaked back. He was very pleased to have a visitor. Now he wouldn't be bored while he was waiting for Chloe to come home. "I'm Pogo."

"And I'm Pip," replied Pip. He was starting to feel a lot better. He looked around the guinea-pig's hutch. It was very different to his cage. It was a lot bigger, and there wasn't a wheel to run around in. And Pogo didn't have a little plastic house to sleep in, like Pip did. Instead, he had a big pile of rather prickly hay.

"Do you mind if I have a look around?" Pip asked.

Pogo watched as Pip ran all around the hutch, snuffling into every corner. He made Pogo feel quite dizzy. "Would you like something to eat?" Pogo squeaked. "Or a drink of water?"

Pip paused and looked curiously at Pogo. "What kind of things do you eat?"

Pogo blinked. "I've got some sunflower seeds. They're my favourite things – you can have some if you want. My food bowl is out in the run."

Pip loved sunflower seeds too. And he

was a bit thirsty. He peered nervously out of the hutch. "I think we're safe. That cat has gone," he squeaked. "Let's go!"

Pogo trotted behind him into the sunshine. He liked having someone to share things with. And he had never met anyone like Pip before. The little hamster was so full of energy!

As Pip took a sip of water from Pogo's water bottle, he began to feel anxious again. What if Rashid had noticed that his cage was empty? He would be getting very worried by now.

Chapter Four

"I'd better go home," Pip told Pogo. "The cat's gone now. I *must* get back before Rashid finds out I'm missing. He's my owner."

"No, you can't go yet," Pogo squeaked in alarm.

"Why not?" Pip asked. He liked the guinea-pig a lot, but he knew that Rashid would be worried about him.

"Look over there," Pogo squeaked quietly. "By the big tree."

Puzzled, Pip looked across the garden.

For a moment, he couldn't see anything at all. Then he spotted the tip of a stripy tail, poking out from behind the tree.

"Doris is still there," Pogo explained. "You can't leave yet."

"Oh dear." Pip hadn't spotted the cat until now. He nuzzled his nose against Pogo's shiny smooth fur. "It's lucky you saw her. Cats and hamsters don't get on!" he squeaked.

"Come and have something to eat," Pogo suggested, leading Pip over to his food bowl. "Chloe filled my bowl up this morning."

"Good! I love sunflower seeds!" squeaked Pip. He still felt a bit full from the seeds he'd found in the flowerbed, so he decided to save Pogo's seeds for later.

He started stuffing them into his cheek pouches, one by one.

Pogo couldn't believe his eyes. "What *are* you doing?" he squeaked, as the little hamster's cheeks got bigger and bigger.

"What's the matter?" Pip mumbled through a mouthful of seeds. "I'm just saving these for later. Is that OK?"

"Of course," Pogo squeaked. "Have as

many as you want." But he couldn't help thinking that the hamster looked very funny!

Pip shifted the seeds in his cheeks so that they felt more comfortable. "Your cage is really different to mine," he told Pogo. "I have sawdust in the bottom of my cage, and a little house full of soft wool to sleep in."

"Well, I sleep in a lovely pile of hay," Pogo replied. "It's very warm and cosy."

"Where's your wheel?" Pip asked, looking round. "What do you do when you want to run about?"

Pogo was puzzled. "I come out here in my run," he explained. "I've got lots of room."

"Yes, but don't you wish you had some

things to play with?" Pip scurried up and down the grass a few times, and then stopped. "I can slide down tunnels and climb up ladders in *my* cage."

"Oh." Pogo wasn't sure he liked the sound of that at all. "Guinea-pigs don't do that sort of thing."

"Hamsters do!" Pip squeaked. "I love running around all the time. That's why I like my wheel so much. I can run for as long as I like."

"But where do you run *to*?" Pogo asked.

"Nowhere!" Pip squeaked in surprise.

Pogo thought that sounded rather odd. But he didn't say so.

A breeze blew through the run, ruffling their fur, and Pip shivered. "Do you always stay outside, Pogo?" he asked.

"Most of the time," Pogo replied cheerfully. "Chloe takes me into the house sometimes, but I love my hutch and my run best of all. When I am indoors my claws sometimes get caught on the carpet. Living outside is much nicer. The grass is lovely and cool under my paws."

Pip shuddered. "I wouldn't like it very much," he squeaked.

"But it's lovely," Pogo told him eagerly. "There's lots of space, and at night I can look up at the stars."

"It's getting dark now," Pip squeaked miserably, staring up at the sky. "Pogo, what *am* I going to do?"

"You'll have to stay here with me," Pogo said firmly. "Doris might still be hanging around."

"But—" Pip began. Then there was a loud bang and he froze. "What's that noise?"

"It's just the back door." Pogo could see that his new friend was really frightened. "It must be Chloe, coming to see me."

Pip scuttled into the hutch, and jumped into the pile of hay. He buried himself right out of sight.

"Pip, what's the matter?" Pogo hurried after him. He nudged the rustling hay with his nose. "You mustn't be scared of Chloe. She's really nice."

Pip popped his head out of the hay.

One wisp dangled from his ear. "Yes,
but what if she sees me?" he squeaked.
"She won't know I live next door. She
might take me to a pet shop or something. Then I'd *never* see Rashid
again."

Pogo realised that Pip was right. So he
patted the hay with his paw until the
hamster was completely hidden. Then
he trotted out to see Chloe. She'd

brought him a handful of parsley as a
special treat.

"Sorry we didn't get a chance to play
today, Pogo," Chloe said, opening the
door of the run and lifting the guinea-
pig on to her lap. "Mum took me
shopping after school."

From underneath the prickly hay, Pip
could hear Chloe talking to Pogo. She
sounded very kind. Pip wanted to see
what she looked like, so he poked his
head out of the hay just a little. Pogo
was sitting on Chloe's lap while she knelt
on the lawn. She was stroking the
guinea-pig gently.

Pip suddenly felt very sad and lonely.
Sometimes Rashid let Pip sit on his
shoulder while he did his homework.

Rashid *must* have noticed that he was missing by now. Pip wished he could be at home again.

Chloe put Pogo back into the run, and went back inside her house. Pogo hurried over to Pip. The hamster looked utterly miserable. His nose had stopped twitching and his little ears were lying down flat. "Don't worry, Pip," squeaked Pogo. "You can stay here with me for as long as you like."

"Thank you." Pip tried his best to sound cheerful. "But I know Rashid will be looking for me. I just *have* to get home somehow."

Chapter Five

"Go to sleep, Pip," Pogo squeaked
gently. Pip was scurrying up and down
the run, trying to spot Doris the cat. But
it was getting too dark to see anything.

"I can't," Pip squeaked unhappily.
"Maybe I should just make a run for it.
If I can't see Doris, then she can't see *me*
either."

"No, you mustn't do that," Pogo
warned him. "Cats can see very well in
the dark. And anyway, how will you get
into the house?"

"The same way I got out." His mind made up, Pip rushed over to the hole in the wire mesh and began squeezing through it. "I'll go in through the kitchen door. Thank you very much for helping me, Pogo. But I *must* go home now. Rashid will be waiting for me."

"But the kitchen door will be closed," Pogo pointed out.

Pip stopped halfway through the hole. He hadn't thought of that.

"It's getting late and it's dark and cold," Pogo went on. "People don't leave their doors open at night."

"Rashid might have left it open for me," Pip squeaked hopefully.

"But he doesn't even know you're outside," Pogo told him.

Pogo was right, Pip thought sadly. He wouldn't be able to get into the house now. And tomorrow, Doris would be prowling around again . . . "What *am* I going to do, Pogo?" he wailed. The air had turned much colder now and the grass felt damp under his paws. Pip started shivering.

"You're getting cold," Pogo squeaked.

"Come on, let's go inside and get some sleep."

Pip didn't argue any more. It *was* cold and the dark was very scary.

Suddenly, a large brown shape with a long bushy tail ran across the bottom of the garden. Pip leaped in the air with fright. "That's not Doris!" he squeaked. "It's too big to be a cat."

"It was a fox," Pogo told him.

Pip thought he sounded very cheerful, considering there was a huge creature roaming around. "A fox? What's that?"

"It's a bit like a dog," Pogo explained. "Don't worry, he can't get in here." He nudged the quivering hamster into the hutch. "Come on, we can make a cosy nest in the hay."

Pip lay down in the hay close to Pogo. At least it was a bit warmer in here. But still not as warm as the snug little house in his cage. Just as he was dozing off, a loud noise made him jump to his paws again.

Whoo! Whoo!

"What's that?" Pip squeaked in alarm.

"It's only an owl," Pogo replied.

"That's a big bird. It's all right, we're safe in here."

Pip closed his eyes very tight and tried to go to sleep. It was really scary being outdoors in the dark, even with Pogo beside him. Pip wished with all his heart that he was safely tucked up in his cage in Rashid's new bedroom.

Pogo woke up first the next morning. The sun was shining on to the roof of the hutch, making Pogo's black and brown fur feel nice and warm. He looked over at Pip. The hamster was still fast asleep, curled into a tight, golden ball.

Pogo stretched and got to his feet. He wondered if Pip would make it home today. Doris was probably already out on her morning prowl. The greedy cat would be on the watch for Pip all the time now, that was for sure. Pogo sighed to himself. He knew Pip had to go back to his owner. But it was lovely having a friend while Chloe was at school.

His ears pricked up as he heard someone talking in the garden. Chloe was coming to see him. Maybe she was bringing him something tasty for his breakfast. Some more parsley perhaps, or a juicy piece of cucumber. Pogo licked his lips and trotted out into the run. To his surprise, he saw that Chloe had someone else with her, a boy who was about the same age.

"I just don't know where Pip's got to,"

the boy was saying sadly. "He got out of his cage yesterday and I haven't seen him since."

Pip? Out of his cage? Pogo could hardly believe his ears. He raced back into the hutch. "Pip! Wake up!" he squeaked at the top of his voice.

Pip yawned. "What's the matter?" he squeaked sleepily.

"There's a boy outside with Chloe. I think it's Rashid!" Pogo was so excited, he jumped all around the hutch.

"Rashid?" Pip's eyes opened wide. His nose twitched rapidly, making his whiskers tremble. He scrambled out of the hay and ran outside. "Rashid!" he squeaked. "Here I am!"

chapter Six

"Rashid!" Pip was running so fast, he almost went head over heels. "Don't go without me!"

Rashid was still talking to Chloe. When he heard Pip squeaking, he looked round and his face lit up. "Pip!" he gasped.

Chloe opened the hutch, and Rashid scooped the hamster up in his hand. He stared at Pip as if he couldn't believe his eyes. "What are *you* doing here?"

Chloe looked just as amazed as

Rashid. "How did your hamster get into Pogo's cage?" she asked.

"Well, it's a long story," Pip squeaked excitedly. He ran up Rashid's arm and sat on his shoulder. "But Pogo looked after me. He's my *best* friend!"

"Oh, I didn't do much really," Pogo called back from the run. He was pleased that Pip had found his owner again. But he couldn't help feeling rather sad too. Now Pip would go home with Rashid, back to his own cage. Pogo realised he might not see the little hamster again. After all, Pip lived indoors. He wouldn't come out into the garden very often.

Chloe lifted Pogo out of the hutch too. She and Rashid carried on talking, trying to work out how Pip had got into Pogo's cage.

"I suppose you'll be glad to go back home, Pip," Pogo squeaked across to Pip. He tried to sound cheerful.

"Yes, I will," Pip agreed, but then he felt a bit upset. "I don't want to leave you, though, Pogo. I'll miss you."

"I'll miss you too," Pogo squeaked. He watched gloomily as Rashid walked back up the garden, with Pip still on his shoulder.

Pip turned back to look at Pogo. "Goodbye, Pogo," he squeaked. "I'll never forget you."

"And I'll never forget *you*," Pogo replied.

Pip finished the seed he was eating, and glanced round Rashid's bedroom. It still looked rather untidy, with boxes everywhere. But it was a lovely room with a big window to let in the sunshine. His cage was on a table right by the window. Pip really liked it.

It was good to be home, he thought.

He ran up one of the ladders in his cage and slid down a tunnel. Then he scampered over to his wheel and ran round for a while. But he couldn't stop thinking about Pogo. He wondered what his friend was doing now.

"And where *has* Rashid got to?" he thought. Rashid had promised to let Pip

out of his cage for a while. But the doorbell had rung and he had gone downstairs to see who it was.

Pip ran faster in his wheel. It made a loud whirring sound. Then he heard another noise. Footsteps were coming up the stairs. Rashid was coming back, and it sounded like there was someone with him.

Pip felt very curious. He stopped running round in his wheel and listened hard. The bedroom door opened. Rashid came in, followed by Chloe. And she was holding Pogo!

"Pogo!" Pip squealed with delight. He hopped off his wheel and raced over to the side of his cage. "What are you doing here?"

"Chloe has come to play with Rashid," Pogo explained as Chloe carried him across the room and stood next to the table.

"And you've come to play with me too!" Pip went mad with joy. He darted about all over his cage, kicking up clouds of sawdust with his paws. "Look, I'll let you have a go on my wheel if you like." And he jumped back on to it, and ran round as fast as he could.

"Thank you," squeaked Pogo. "But I don't think I'll fit!"

"Never mind," Pip squeaked back, as Rashid lifted him out of the cage. "I'll race you across the carpet instead, as long as your claws don't get stuck!" As soon as Rashid put him down on the table, Pip dashed over to Chloe and stretched up to give Pogo a friendly sniff.

Pogo felt very happy. He wriggled so much that Chloe put him on the floor. Rashid put Pip down next to him.

Pip nudged Pogo with his nose, his whiskers trembling with excitement.

Pogo looked at Pip. "Ready, steady, go!" he squeaked. And off they raced.

Snowflake and Sparkle

Snowflake is a puppy with big paws and soft, golden fur. His best friend is Sparkle – a very unusual kitten. She chases balls, scares the postman and begs for treats – just like a dog!

Snowflake longs to be more like Sparkle – but one day, the tiny kitten gets into BIG trouble. Can Snowflake come to the rescue?

Minty and Monty

Monty is a little puppy with big plans. He wants to be a top sheepdog, just like his mum. But there's one problem – Monty is scared of sheep.

A lamb called Minty might be able to help. Minty isn't scared of anything! She knows how to make Monty the perfect sheepdog – but first she has to make him her friend . . .

Look out for **Best▾Friends** No 4

Carrot and Clover

Carrot is a little rabbit who lives in Becky's garden with his best friend Clover, a fluffy yellow chick. Every morning, Becky gives them their breakfast – then she goes out of the gate, and doesn't come back until teatime.

Carrot and Clover have never been outside the gate – let alone to school, where Becky spends the day! One day they decide to follow her – and find a whole new world waiting for them . . .

More Jenny Dale titles!

The prices shown below are correct at the time of going to press. However, Macmillan Publishers reserve the right to show new retail prices on covers which may differ from those previously advertised.

JENNY DALE'S BEST FRIENDS

1. Snowflake and Sparkle	0 330 39853 9	£3.50
2. Pogo and Pip	0 330 39854 7	£3.50
3. Minty and Monty	0 330 39855 5	£3.50

JENNY DALE'S PUPPY TALES™

1. Gus the Greedy Puppy	0 330 37359 5	£2.99
2. Lily the Lost Puppy	0 330 37360 9	£2.99
3. Spot the Sporty Puppy	0 330 37361 7	£2.99
4. Lenny the Lazy Puppy	0 330 37362 5	£2.99

JENNY DALE'S KITTEN TALES™

1. Star the Snowy Kitten	0 330 37451 6	£2.99
2. Bob the Bouncy Kitten	0 330 37452 4	£2.99
3. Felix the Fluffy Kitten	0 330 37453 2	£2.99
4. Nell the Naughty kitten	0 330 37454 0	£2.99

All Macmillan titles can be ordered at your local bookshop
or are available by post from:

Book Service by Post
PO Box 29, Douglas, Isle of Man IM99 1BQ

Credit cards accepted. For details:
Telephone: 01624 675137
Fax: 01624 670923
E-mail: bookshop@enterprise.net

Free postage and packing in the UK.
Overseas customers: add £1 per book (paperback)
and £3 per book (hardback).